All Aboard

Monorail Trains

by Jenna Lee Gleisner

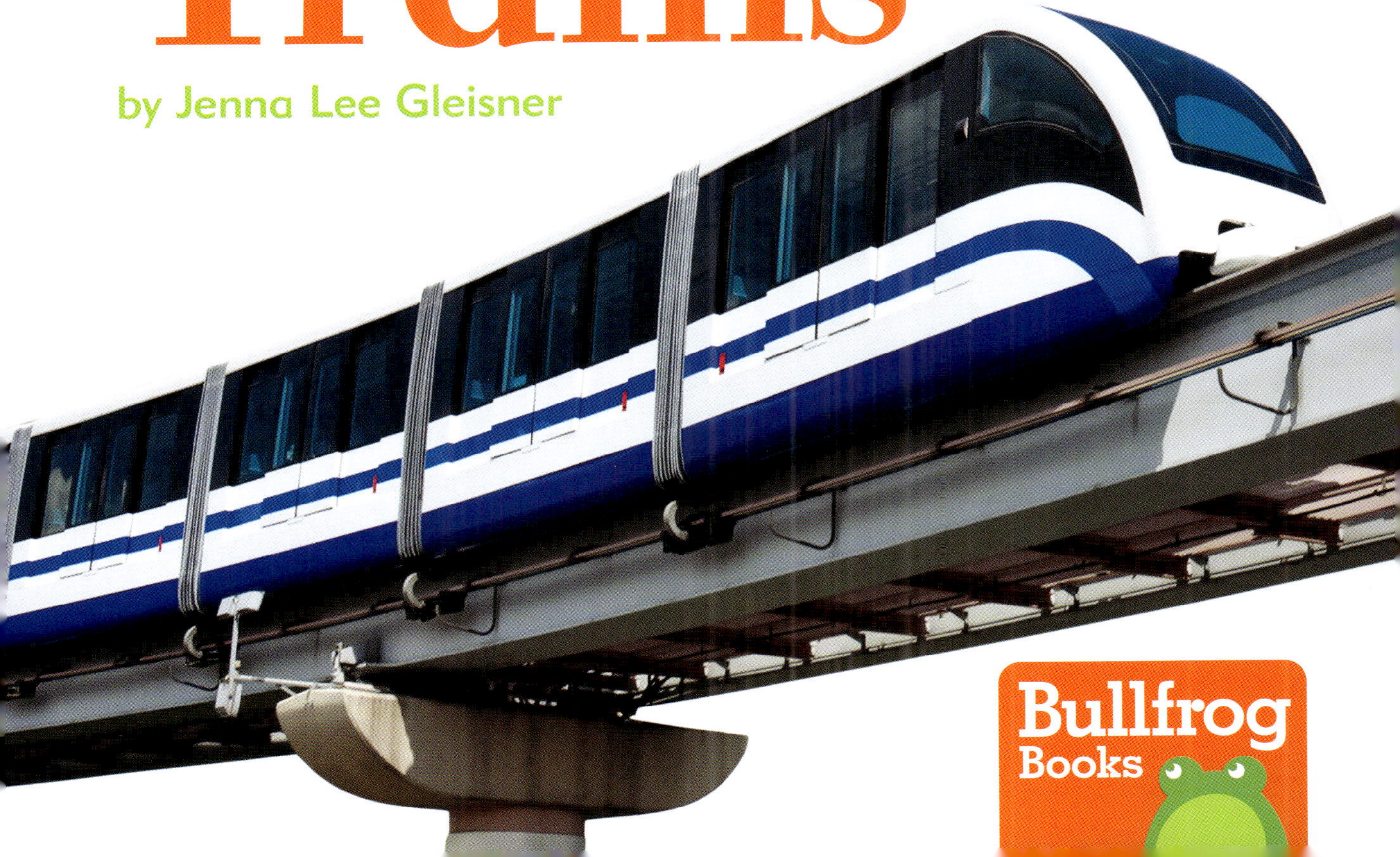

Bullfrog Books

Ideas for Parents and Teachers

Bullfrog Books let children practice reading informational text at the earliest reading levels. Repetition, familiar words, and photo labels support early readers.

Before Reading

- Discuss the cover photo. What does it tell them?
- Look at the picture glossary together. Read and discuss the words.

Read the Book

- "Walk" through the book and look at the photos. Let the child ask questions. Point out the photo labels.
- Read the book to the child, or have him or her read independently.

After Reading

- Prompt the child to think more. Ask: Have you ever ridden on a monorail train? Where was it?

Bullfrog Books are published by Jump!
5357 Penn Avenue South
Minneapolis, MN 55419
www.jumplibrary.com

Library of Congress Cataloging-in-Publication Data

Names: Gleisner, Jenna Lee, author.
Title: Monorail trains / Jenna Lee Gleisner.
Description: Minneapolis, MN: Jump!, Inc., [2020]
Series: All aboard | Includes index.
Audience: Ages 5–8 | Audience: Grades K–1
Identifiers: LCCN 2019022734 (print)
LCCN 2019022735 (ebook)
ISBN 9781645272441 (hardcover)
ISBN 9781645272458 (ebook)
Subjects: LCSH: Monorail railroads
United States—Juvenile literature.
Classification: LCC TF694 .G54 2020 (print)
LCC TF694 (ebook) | DDC 388.4/2—dc23
LC record available at https://lccn.loc.gov/2019022734
LC ebook record available at https://lccn.loc.gov/2019022735

Editors: Jenna Trnka and Sally Hartfiel
Designer: Molly Ballanger

Photo Credits: amirulsyaidi/iStock, cover; Sailorr/Shutterstock, 1; velirina/Shutterstock, 3; Bayurov Alexander/Shutterstock, 4, 23tr; Javier Larrea/Age Fotostock, 5, 23tl; Alexander Gatsenko/Shutterstock, 6–7, 23bl; Hanna Alandi/Shutterstock, 8; ClaraNila/iStock, 9; Christian Ohde/imageBROKER/SuperStock, 10–11; Michael Willis/Alamy, 12–13; Lucy Clark/Dreamstime, 14–15, 23br; vewfinder/Shutterstock, 16; drial7m1/iStock, 17; Ceri Breeze/Shutterstock, 18–19; Bea Cooper/Alamy, 20–21; smodi/iStock, 24.

Printed in the United States of America at Corporate Graphics in North Mankato, Minnesota.

Table of Contents

One Rail

Have you seen a monorail train?

Maybe you have been on one!

rail

These trains use one rail.

This one sits on top of a rail.

This one hangs from a rail!

These trains do not go very fast.

They go slower so we can see.

This one is in a zoo.

We see animals.

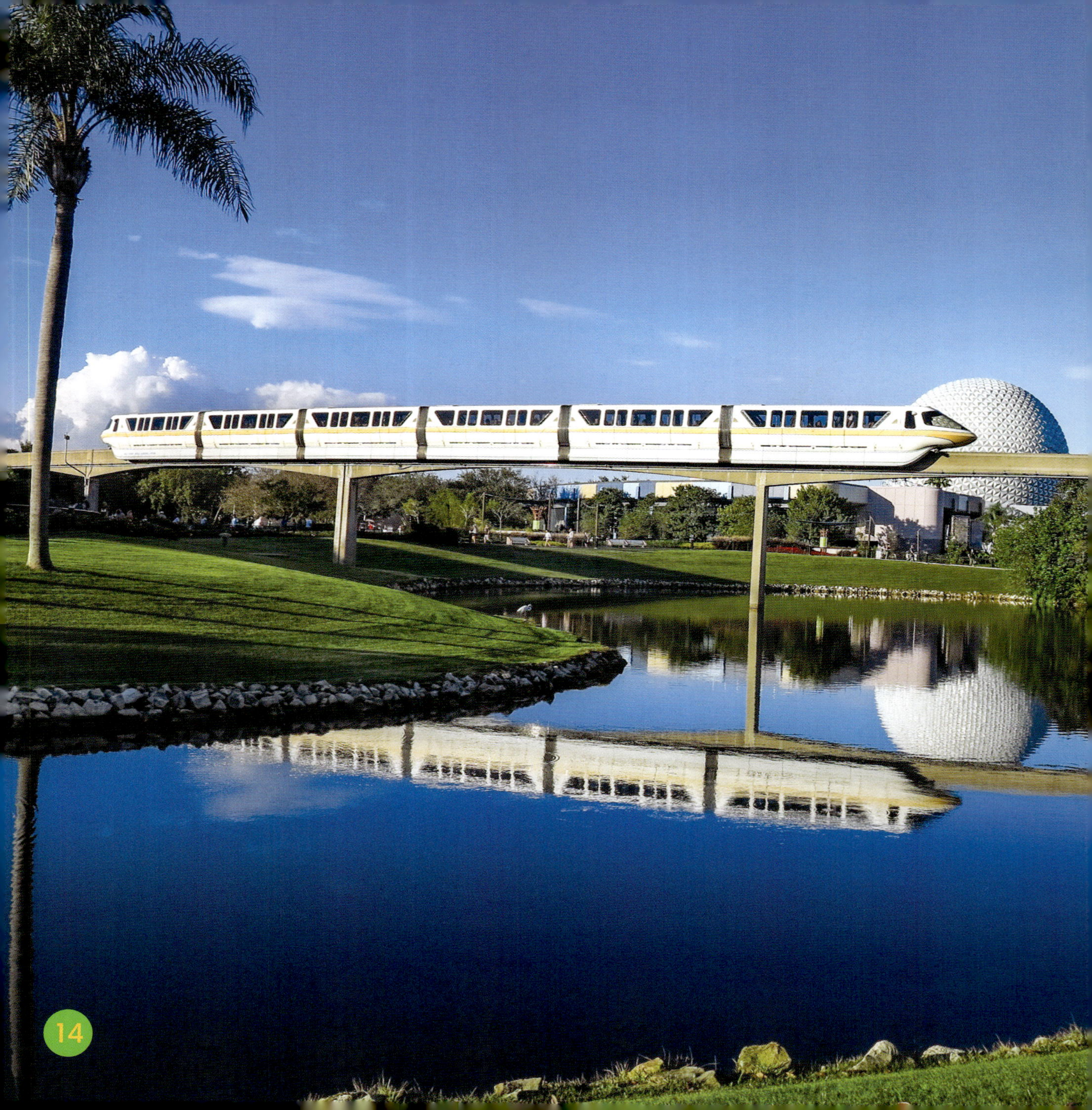

This one is in a theme park.

It is in Walt Disney World!

Fun!

This one is in Seattle.

Seattle, Washington

We can see the city.

driver

We can sit by the driver.

Cool!

All aboard!

Monorails in the United States

Monorails are mostly at theme parks, zoos, and airports. Have you been on any of these monorails in the United States? Are any near you?

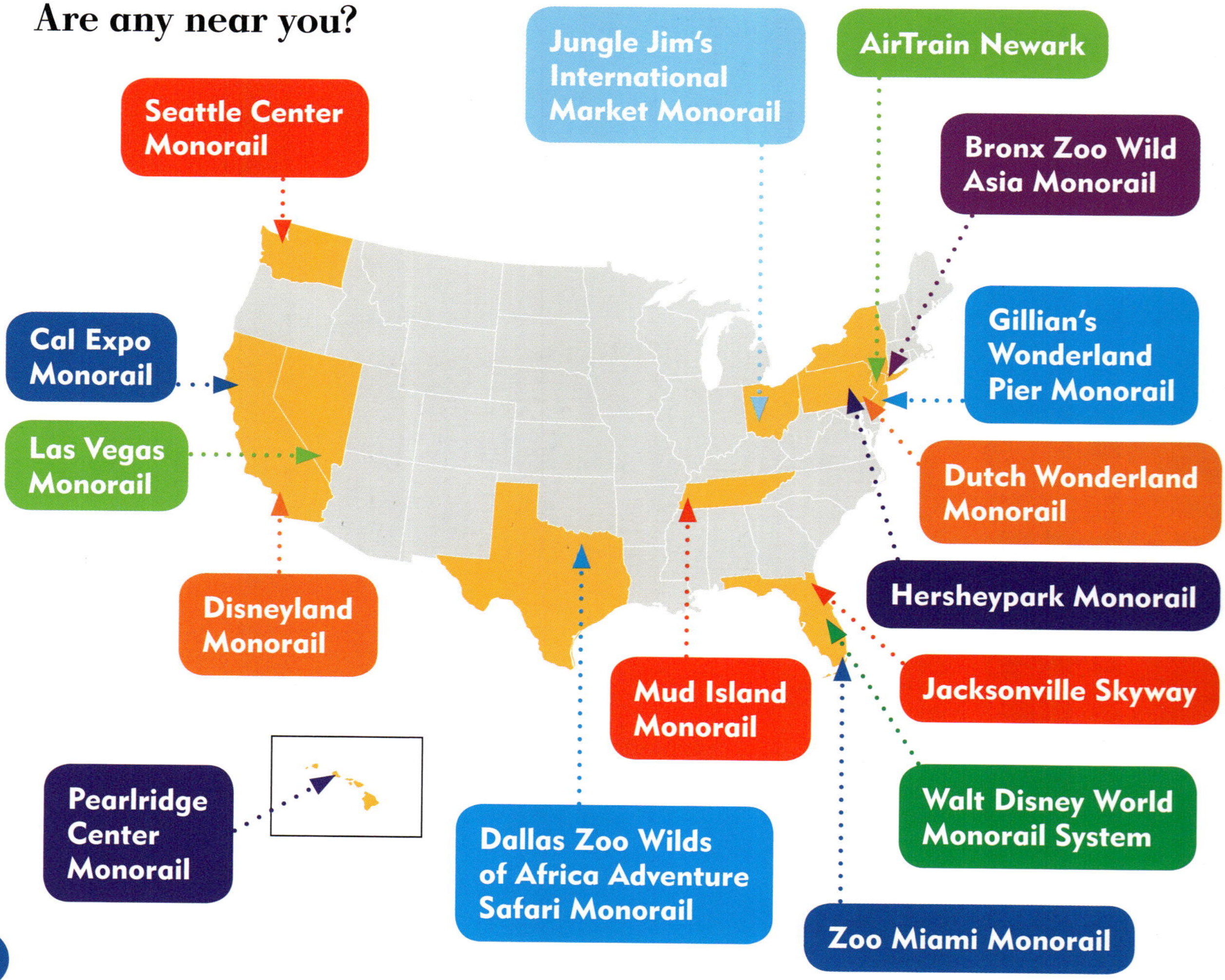

Picture Glossary

aboard
On or onto a train, ship, or aircraft.

monorail train
A train that runs on one rail, either hanging from it or balanced on it.

rail
A bar of steel that forms a track for wheeled vehicles, like trains.

theme park
An amusement park in which the structures and rides are based on a theme.

Index

To Learn More

Finding more information is as easy as 1, 2, 3.

1. Go to www.factsurfer.com
2. Enter "monorailtrains" into the search box.
3. Choose your book to see a list of websites.